PUFFIN BOOKS

UK | USA | Canada | Ireland | Australia | India | New Zealand | South Africa

Puffin Books is part of the Penguin Random House group of companies
whose addresses can be found at global.penguinrandomhouse.com.

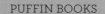
puffinbooks.com

First published 2015

001

Characters and artwork are the original creation of Tove Jansson

Written by Richard Dungworth

Text and illustrations copyright © Moomin Characters™, 2015

A CIP catalogue record for this book is available from the British Library

Made and printed in China

Hardback ISBN: 978-0-141-35981-6

Paperback ISBN: 978-0-141-35993-9

MOOMIN
and the
Wishing Star

BASED ON THE ORIGINAL STORIES BY

Tove Jansson

PUFFIN

Summer was drifting lazily towards autumn in Moominvalley. The days were becoming a little shorter and a little cooler.

Moomintroll had spent the afternoon exploring and had discovered the perfect spot to enjoy the fine weather while it lasted. It was a quiet, sheltered pool near the foot of a mountain.

"Pee-hoo!"

sang Moomin contentedly as he bathed.

Then something caught his eye –
a small white something glistening just
below the surface of the water.

Moomintroll fished the something out. It was a little pebble, perfectly round and perfectly smooth. Moomin turned it over in his hands, gazing at it admiringly. It had a silvery-white gleam that seemed almost magical.

"What a treasure!"
thought Moomin.

Eager to show his friends, Moomin
climbed out of the pool, shook himself dry
and hurried back to the Moominhouse.

Moomin arrived home to find everyone outside on the verandah, having supper. He proudly showed them his pebble.

"Oh! It's beautiful!" said Snorkmaiden. "Look how it shines – like starlight!" Her eyes widened with wonder. "Imagine if that's what it is! A fallen star . . ."

At this, Sniff became so excited he dropped the syrup spoon. "If it *is* a fallen star," he cried, "it'll give you a *wish*, Moomintroll!"

The mention of a wish led to great excitement. Snorkmaiden clapped her hands, laughing gleefully.

"I know what I'd wish for," she said. "An elegant silver tail-ring!"

"Emeralds!" cried Sniff, hopping from one foot to the other. "Or perhaps diamonds! No – a treasure chest, filled with gemstones!"

Moomintroll stared at his pebble. Could it be a star? If it *was*, how would he decide on a wish?

He gave a little jump as Moominmamma
touched him on the shoulder.

"Remember that it is *your* wish, Moomintroll,"
she murmured. "No one else can tell you
what to wish for."

Moomin nodded and slipped away
to the quiet of his room to give the
matter some serious thought.

But the more Moomintroll thought,
the harder he found it to choose a wish.
Was it wrong to use it for himself?
He imagined how delighted Snorkmaiden
would be with a shiny new tail-ring.

"Or perhaps a rose bush for Mamma's
garden?" thought Moomin. "Or bookends
for Pappa . . ."

The night got darker and darker and Moomin
rubbed his eyes. Was it his imagination,
or was his pebble getting darker too?

"If I don't make up my mind soon,
its shine will be gone –
         and the wish too!" he fretted.
So Moomin did as he always
did when faced with a
difficult problem . . .

         he went to visit Snufkin.

Moomin found his friend sitting by his campfire, playing a tune on his accordian. He stopped as Moomintroll approached and spoke kindly, "Sit down, old chap, and tell me what's on your mind."

Moomin told Snufkin all about finding the pebble, and Snorkmaiden and Sniff thinking it was a wishing star, and about how hard it was deciding what to wish for.

"And now, look – its shine is fading! Do you think the wish will work?"

Moomin passed the star pebble to Snufkin, who inspected it closely. "Well, I'm no expert," he said. "Wishes are tricky things. But it *does* look like it's fading, and I don't think you'll be able to wish on a faded star."

"As for how to get the shine back, sometimes things just need to be where they belong."

"You mean, I should put it back?" said Moomin. "That might help?"

Snufkin nodded. "And then you can make your wish," he said.

Moomintroll led the way to the little pool where he had found the star pebble. As they drew near, he let out a cry. "Snufkin! Look! It's *full* of stars!"

The water's smooth surface reflected the night sky above. It sparkled with countless tiny, twinkling lights.

"Now," said Snufkin. "Drop the pebble in and make your wish."

Moomin admired his special pebble one last time, then let it drop . . .

p l o p !

. . . into the water.
The ripples died away and the mirrored stars settled down once more. He gazed into the pool rather sadly. Then his heart leapt as a streak of silver raced across the water.

"A shooting star!" gasped Moomintroll.
They both looked up eagerly. "There's another!
And another! Oh, Snufkin," he continued,
without thinking, "I wish everyone were
here with us to see them!"

"There you are," said Snufkin.
"That's your wish!"

Moomin was taken aback. "Was it?" he asked.
"I hardly noticed. How will it come true?"
"Oh, it's very tricky to tell with wishes.
You'll have to wait and see," said Snufkin.

They watched the stars together
for some time. At last, tired but happy,
they made their way home.

At breakfast the next morning, Moomin told everyone to prepare for a secret expedition that night.

"Oh, Moomintroll!" cried Snorkmaiden. "Where are we going? Is this to do with your wish?"

But Moomin wouldn't say anything. He only smiled.

"How lovely, dear," said Moominmamma. "I'll make a plum cake."

Moomin's tummy felt more and more tingly all day as they packed up a picnic and blankets and waited for the sun to set.

Nightfall seemed to take a very long time to come.

That night, the whole family gathered by Moomintroll's pool. Moomin was so excited that he couldn't sit still and he barely nibbled at his slice of plum cake.

But the night got later and later, and no shooting stars appeared. Moomin's tummy felt more tingly than ever before.

Moominmamma noticed his ears drooping, and asked him what was wrong.

"Oh, Mamma, it's my wish! I saw the most amazing shooting stars and I wished that everyone could see them too – but I must have made the wish wrong and now it's lost forever!" cried Moomin.

Moominmamma stroked his head.

"Oh, Moomintroll, my Moomintroll, don't be upset. Wishes are very tricky things. Maybe it will come true tomorrow night?"

Just then, a shining star streaked across the sky.
    "Did you see that?" gasped Snorkmaiden.
"Look, there's another one!"
    "And another! Look! Look!" cried Sniff.

Moomin clapped his hands with delight before lying back on the ground to gaze at the stars. "My wish did come true, after all," he whispered.

"Thank you for using your wish for us, Moomin!"
said Snorkmaiden. "I've never seen
anything so beautiful."

"Well done, my Moomintroll,"
said Moominmamma softly, packing up
the last of the picnic things.

And Moomin felt warm and lucky and
very, *very* happy as together they made
their way back to the Moominhouse
in the pale early-morning light.

The End